# The MVP

## LaRone Randolph

# Table of Contents

# Forward

I want to thank my Mom, Dad, Brothers and Sister
for always believing in me. Love,

LaRone

# INTRODUCTION

Competition is usually meant to only push someone harder. When being pushed hard it can sometimes lead to big risks and that can result in failure, but you must never give up or give in. We all take risk just choose wisely.

## Players

- LaRone (The MVP)
- Freeman
- Hawkins
- Eleazer
- Yair
- Drew
- Hicks

## Coach

- Ibarra

## Commentators

- Chuck Kody

# THE OVERCOMING

Here it is Game 7 Larone has 40 points alone, the Score 120 to 122 with 45 seconds on the clock left. Los Angeles Lions shoot the three they make it"! "Boston Cubs coming up the court they want to slow the game down to get the clutch shot off." The score is 125 to 123 Lions are down by 2, Coach Ibarra is yelling "run the ISO play," he wants to run the play, so they can get the shot off.

"LaRone comes down the court he runs the ISO play, 10 seconds on the clock he goes to the basket and falls hard. He's hurt! It's a sprained ankle! This is bad the last 5 seconds of the game, they've lost this championship! The game is over! The Cubs win the championship.

LaRone is out of the game because of his injury it's really not looking good he will probably be out for a month or maybe the rest of his career, "Chuck said.

LaRone Started thinking to himself ....

Man! I tried hard and played even harder, yet we lost the game. I've always lead my team this time I was hurt badly, and I feel like I let them down. The off-season was about to start which would give me time to heal. I wonder what was going to happen now that I've gotten hurt? I need to heal fast before I'm out! Thank God, we're headed into the off-season! I know that things are about to change.

# THE
# GATHERING

After the finals my team the Lions decided to pick up a dominant scorer named Eleazer. This is a big change for us he will be starting as shooting guard. All I can think about is, if I don't recover they won't start me as point guard. The coaches are starting to pick new players they also ended up picking a small forward superstar. This guy is a very good all-around player, a defensive monster, 3pt specialist and a very good re-bounder his name is Stewart. I've seen him on the court and he has skills. After the coaches and owners picked the new players; we all got a chance to get to know each other. I had been a little worried but I'm confident that the team still needs me. Right? I started my recovery on July 20th I expected a 30-day recovery after seeing my doctor who said I was progressing very well. So, I know that I will be at it again soon. I had received news former MVP Drew Miguel might come to join our team as well. It's great that there are so many changes going on, but I really want to get back to the game.

As time passed by August 19th came quickly, my doctor said I'm healed and I am able to get back at it for the first day of practice! I'm so excited! So, the decision was made, and Drew Miguel joined us who is now going to be one of the starters. We are decked out for the bench we also picked up Freeman, Hawkins, and Hicks. The team is coming together. I just have to make sure that I'm ready and good to go. Coach Ibarra calls the team for practice, we all go to the Lions practice facility. We worked on our ISO (isolation) plays, and clutch plays. It seemed that our team had come together perfectly.

The new season was near, and we're prepared for this season's opening game. One of our first games will be a rematch against the Boston Cubs. Let's Get it!

# I'M NOT DONE YET

The game is about to kick off The Boston Cubs versus The Los Angeles Lions! As I was thinking to myself I flashed back to my horrible injury that left me devastated at the end of our finals. I told myself not again! We will make it this season to the finals once again, then to the championship! Yes, we can do it! No, we will do it!

Let's Get it! I said.

"Tip-off is about to begin the Lions are ready to begin we are ready to win this! Larone goes for the three-pointer and makes it. Now as he was coming down the court Larone passes the ball to Eleazar he hits an alley-oop and dunks it! "Let's get it!" Larone yells. 1st quarter ended with a score of 45 to 20, 2nd quarter begins, here we go. They are rocking it" Chuck said, 70 to 40 Lions in the lead.

Coach Ibarra calls a timeout and says "I want to blow them out by 60 were up by 30, we have another half to go to keep it up! Come on guys let's run the ISO (isolation) plays so they won't notice a thing on the court, we'll get Freeman in and Hawkins. Let's start shooting some three- pointers alright!"

Now the half is over the score 81 to 41. The reporters are surprised that it's 81 to 41, Chuck says "If the Boston Cubs keep this up then they will not win the finals or even make the finals." Going into the 2nd half, we are way in the lead! It's crazy! It's such a huge blowout. The question is if they can keep this up during the entire season. It's gonna be hard but we can do it! Chuck says with excitement "The Lions are coming down the court and they're going to shoot a three! They made it! Larone is on fire from the perimeter he hits 8 three-pointers in a row, he's now at 24 points! Wow!"

We have scored 37 points in the quarter. now we have 118 on the board, coach Ibarra says, "This game is very far apart keep it up guys, don't get cocky though! Keep playing hard till the game ends, we got these guys we're up by 72 points! Good job guys! Let's keep running those plays and this will be easy as practice, this game is in our hands!". 4th quarter comes around, and we score 39 more points and The Boston Cubs only score 1 point! 110 the game is over we've won! This was the Biggest blowout in

NBA history this rematch for us is one for the books sweet victory! Even though they lost we let them know it was a good game and they did a good job.

We're now ten games in and undefeated! As we get ready to play The Houston Rollers, it's crunch time! The game is going good yet we're down by 7 trying to find a way out of this. Now our game plan is to shoot two three-pointers and draw a foul to try to tie the game or win the game. Coach Ibarra says, "Run the clutch play on offense and for defense to run the cheese play". I said, "we got these guys we can win this game trust me, I know we can do this!"

Here we go 22.6 seconds left we have the ball. I'm coming down the court and pass the ball to Yair goes for the three and misses. There is 10 seconds left I shoot for a three and got fouled I missed the three pointers. That would've been a four-point play but three free throws coming up. The first shot is good, second is good and the third shot is great! 7.6 seconds on the clock. Houston has the ball I get the steal and go for the three, it's good! Fans started yelling "that was a foul on the play!" The refs went back to look at the play, they came back one free throw for us. Now, the score is 123 to 122. Now, I'm at the free through line I shoot and make it, the crowd roars! It's now a tie game! "The Lions will go back court", arena voice says" the Lions will be advancing up the court. We take the ball out and pass the ball in and they don't lay a hand on the ball so, we can't waste any time I pick up the ball and the crowd chants 5, 4, 3 I give it my all and shoot it, the crowd still chanting 2, 1, 0 everyone is staring at the ball while it's in the air; the ball hits the side of the rim. The ball bounces again some Lion's fan in the arena looks at the ball as it's moving up in the air, it's a miracle the ball swished in the basket! The crowd roars and cheers as we win the game and are still undefeated! "The Lions have been playing phenomenal if they keep this up they could beat the 73-9 record by the Golden State Gophers, it would be history, in fact they are playing the Golden State Gophers tomorrow! "says Chuck.

Today is game day Lions vs Golden State Gophers this is the first meeting since they played in the conference finals. Chuck says, "The Lions are the best team in the league right now, maybe even the best team ever to be in the NBA." Kody says, "The game is about to begin this is going to be a really good game! this is gonna be hard as a brick." As the Lions are coming on the floor the crowd is yelling horrible things at us. We're playing at the Chase center in San Francisco. We are prepared for this game, we are seeking this victory we do not want to lose. Tip-off is in our favor. The Gophers are frightened by our performances right now here we get the ball first. We are bringing the ball up court and we shoot and score the three-pointer; eight minutes have passed the quarter is about to be over 1 minute and 23 seconds left in the quarter. The Gophers are bringing the ball up court and the game is tied 43 to 43. The Gophers shoot inside the perimeter and make it 45 to 43 Warriors are up by two. We get the ball, I'm coming up the court at the perimeter I pass the ball to Yair and he puts it in. At the start of the 4th quarter it is 88 to 84 the game is about to start back up again. The Gophers are in the lead. We are now bringing the ball up I pass the ball to Hicks, Hicks passes to Eleazar he alley-oops it to

Yair and he dunks it and gets the 1! One free throw coming up. Yair shoots the free throw and makes it. The Gophers are up by 5, 120 to 115 we are coming down the court and he shoots the three and makes it. They're down by 2 then we steal the ball and dunk it! We tie the game with 1 minute and 4 seconds left. The Gophers bring the ball up and I steal the ball from Steph Murry and I dunk it. 122 to 120 we take the lead! The Gophers bring the ball up court and Steph Murry shoots it and scores! Making it 123 to 122. We call a timeout with 10 seconds left, down by one, we take the ball out. We pass the ball in and I run so fast to the basket I dunk it in with 3 seconds left!

The Gophers pass the ball in and Eleazar steals the ball away from Ken Grant and he shoots the three, swish! He made the basket with 0.7 seconds left. The Gophers pass the ball in and then Yair steals it and the game is over! 50 games later we only lost 7 games our record is 63 and 7. We have the best record in the NBA! We have a game tomorrow against the Brooklyn Nets, we hope to win. We'll be playing the Nets they have lost 63 games and won 7 games they have the worst record in the NBA it may be an easy win. Today, we are ready for the game, bench is starting LeAndre Freeman, Dontay Hicks, and Trey Hawkins also with Eleazar and Drew Miguel.

The game starts we get the ball first I go to the basket and alley-oop to Yair and he dunks. 3 quarters later we are up by 70 points. "It's crazy how this team is so fast, strong, and smart" said Chuck. Then Kody said, "what would they look like during the playoffs," Chuck says, "I don't know but this team looks amazing I think they're going to win the finals, if the Boston Cubs don't get Ant Davis." The 4th quarter is almost over, we have hit 23 three-pointers we're trying to beat the record that the Jackson Cavaliers set, when they scored 25 three-pointers made in a game. Yair shoots the three-pointer and makes it, I bring the ball up court and I shoot the three-pointer as well and I make it! We have now hit 25 three-pointers in a game. We steal the ball from The Brooklyn Nets and Eleazar shoots the three-pointer bang! We have hit 26 three-pointers in a game. We bring the ball in and rush down court, passing the ball to Drew and he shoots it and puts it in! The Nets pass the ball in and Drew pump fakes and shoots it and makes it. I bring them all up the court and I shoot it from the logo and make it in!

The crowd chanted M..V..P.., M..V..P.., I was hyped! Coach called a timeout. Coach Ibarra said, "this game is ours we need that last three-pointers to hit 30 Haha, this is the best night we've had let's keep it up!" 30 seconds left in the game and we take the ball out. We pass the ball in and I pass the ball to Yair and he makes the three-pointer! We have beat the record by 5 three-pointers the new record is set for the NBA. 30 three-pointers in a single game. The game is over. Drew, Yair, Eleazar and myself got to do the post-game interview. First reporter says, "how are you guys so good working together? I responded, "this team bonds very well because we work as team and trust on another." Second reporter asks, "How do you feel about setting a new record in the NBA Andrew?" Drew says, "It feels amazing because it's going be fun to watch other teams try to beat the record!" Five reporters later a someone asks, "Yair and Eleazar how do you feel about being on this team and how do you feel about your winning and losing record?" Yair says "I feel great being on this team it's an amazing feeling to be on this team" then Eleazar says" we are just getting ready for the playoffs. You can learn something from the game whether you win or lose its apart of being an athlete."

# I'M BACK!

We have gone 74-8 this season we have beat the Golden State Gophers record 73-9. We have played against some great teams; Boston Cubs, Golden State Golden State Gophers, Minnesota Vikings, San Antonio Spartans, Chicago Bucks, Oklahoma City Falls, New Haven Jazz. We are doing an amazing job right now. We've swept our way to the western conference finals. We are now facing the Golden State Gophers. They have also swept they're way to the western conference finals. "Both of these teams are very good at what they do, and they both have what it takes to succeed," says Kody. Two games have past, and we have won one game, and the Golden State Gophers have won one game. The 3rd game is about to begin. Three quarters later, we are up by 20 points and we keep scoring! The game is in ours hands. The game is over, we have the lead for the series. Two games later we have won three games and the Golden State Gophers have to win three games in a row to win the series, but we are confident that there will be no stopping us! The 5th game of the series is about to begin. "The Golden State Gophers and the Los Angeles Lions have been working hard this whole series, who is going to get the win?" Chuck said, "obviously the Los Angeles Lions look how they've been carrying themselves I know they are going to win this game!" said Kody. That's exactly what we did, we went on to defeat the Golden State Gophers and move to the finals.

# THE FINALS

The rematch is starting right now The Boston Cubs have made the finals after sweeping everyone in their conference during the playoffs. At the tip-off its Jamaal Hankins, Ky Glass, Al Ford and Ant Darus versus LaRone Randolph, Miguel Jackson, Yair Mammunda and Eleazar Jenkins. The game starts, we win the jump ball. I bring the ball down court and I break Jamaal Hankins ankles followed by an alley-oop to Yair, and he dunks it. Two quarters later we're up by 30 and then went on to win the 1st game of the finals. The second game though, Boston showed no mercy and blew us out by 50 points the score was 125 to 75. Game 3, 1-point game we are down by 1 and we have the ball. Someone passes the ball to me and I shoot the three-pointer and swish it in. The score is now 140 to 138 with the game over. We won the 3rd game! Eleazar had 50 points and Yair had 50 points they both played an excellent game! The next day the team and I went to exercise at the Golden State Gophers practice facility. We learned this new play called, The Mamba. It's one of our best plays yet! The next two days was a very extensive practice, the game was the following night. This is it folks the moment we've been waiting for Game 4! ¨ said Chuck. The ball is in our hands we pass the ball around and Miguel shoots it, he puts the ball in the net from way downtown! Boston went on to win the 4th game. The series of Boston Cubs versus the Los Angeles Lions is tied, 2 games later the series was still tied. There will be a game 7. It will take place at the staples center in Los Angeles. I had tweaked my ankle during practice. I went to the team urgent care and the doctor said "this injury may take a longer time to heal ". I responded angrily" what do u mean this injury may take longer I am not waiting a week our final game is tomorrow and I'm not going to miss it!" I practiced the rest of the day and I learned how to control my injury. It is Friday now one hour till the game and the whole team is practicing. I'm first up on floor and the tip goes to us, first thing I do is shoot it and make the three-pointer, it's good! The score 3 to 12 now, I step back from the three-point line shoot it from long distance and put it in. I pass the ball down to Eleazar and he shoots it and makes it.

Yair taking the ball up court he drives it to the basket and dunks on Jamaal Hankins! Oh, my goodness this is an extreme game! Now, two quarters later the Lions are down by 2; 101 to 103. It's the 4th quarter with 3 minutes left the crowd chanting "defense" very loudly. Eleazar speeding down the court and he posturized Ky Glass and Eleazar says "you ain't got nothing on me ". 31 seconds left Coach Ibarra says, "we got this guy we are down by 5 right now but don't be show- offs because this is one of the best teams in the league we are playing, but we are just as good so let's go out there and show them what we got!". We pass the ball in with the game on the line I pass the ball to Yair he shoots and scores the three-pointer. We are down by 2 now with 15 seconds left The Boston Cubs pass the ball in and Ky dribbling up court and Eleazar steal the ball from Ky and he runs to the basket and he dunks the ball. The crowd is going crazy, Jamaal Hankins coming down the court trying to win the game. We're tied Jamaal Hankins tries a layup. The ball goes up and I'm speeding down the court injured and all, I block Hankins! This game is going into overtime; 112 to 112. The tip-off goes to us and the crowd is chanting, "Let's go Lions!". I speed down the court and posturizes Ant Darus on the drive. The next minute and thirty seconds was a fight, it's a timeout at the moment but I scored 12 points in 30 seconds and I got 8 blocks, my stats are 50 points, 12 rebounds, 15 assist, 9 steals, and 9 blocks I could get a quadruple-double, in fact maybe a legendary double. The game is still on the line and there are twenty-one seconds left they're down by 2. I can make history with the first ever legendary double and 14 three-pointers in a game. The Boston Cubs take the ball out. Ky bringing the ball up court he passes it to Jamaal Hankins and then Hankins passes it to Ant Darius and Darius tries to go for a dunk attempt and I blocked Ant Darius. Boston recovers the ball Ky shoots and gets blocked by me. Boston recovers again they shoot, and I blocked them again. They recover the ball once again I steal it and I shoot the three-pointer and make it. My ankle is hurt again in the finals with the four-point play. I get up and run to the free throw line and shoot the free throw and make it! We are up by 2 with 3 seconds left! Jamaal Hankins tries to shoot the half court, but he's blocked by me again. WE WON! The stats for the game Drew had 15 rebounds, 10 points, Yair had 20 points, 10 rebounds and 10 assist, Eleazar Had 35 points,10 rebounds and 10 blocks. Well as for me I had 53 points, 15 rebounds, 16 assists, 10 steals, and 10 blocks.

# The Awards

The four stars from our team all went to the awards ceremony. The first award was the rookie of the year. The rookie was a dominating scorer he was in the finals and he went wild! The rookie of the year goes to Eleazar Beltran who averaged 21 points and 5 blocks per game. The defensive player of the year was a master of pick pocketing and he averaged 25 points per game and 15 steals per game. This award goes to Yair Mammunda!

The most improved player he was an MVP candidate and a defensive candidate. He was a former MVP, but he got better than that MVP version of himself. The Most improved player goes to, Drew Miguel who averaged 11 blocks per game and 19 points. The MVP award the Most Valuable Player. He Averaged 10 blocks, 39 points, 13 rebounds, 10 steals, 10 assists. The MVP award goes to Jamaal Hankins.... wait, me LaRone Randolph! The Most Valuable player of the year.

# We made history

The Lions go to the finals ten years straight, and I received the MVP all of those years. The Lions went 81-1 in the 9th year and went undefeated in the playoffs to the finals that year. Eleazar got a 400-million-dollar contract to stay with the Lions and Drew got a 230-million-dollar deal. Yair got a 350-million-dollar deal. Then I received a 1-billion-dollar deal. LaRone is the greatest player to ever have played, he got the largest contract broke every record even the 104 points by Wilt Chamberlain. He got 11 rings, 10 MVP's, and he got a rookie of the year he is the greatest player ever to be in the NBA.

HOME **74** 15:16 GUEST **73**

PERIOD **2**

BONUS

BONUS

**8**

**9**

THE MVP